From ACORN to TREE

Camilla de la Bédoyère

Quarto Library

Quarto is the authority on a wide range of topics.

Quarto educates, entertains and enriches the lives of our readers—enthusiasts and lovers of hands-on living.

www.quartoknows.com

This library edition published in 2019 by QEB Publishing, an imprint of The Quarto Group.
6 Orchard Road
Suite 100
Lake Forest, CA 92630
T: +1 949 380 7510
F: +1 949 380 7575
www.QuartoKnows.com

Distributed in the United States and Canada by
Lerner Publisher Services
241 First Avenue North
Minneapolis, MN 55401 U.S.A.
www.lernerbooks.com

A CIP record for this book is available from the Library of Congress.

ISBN 978 0 7112 4369 9

Manufactured in Shenzhen, China PP062019

9 8 7 6 5 4 3 2 1

MIX
Paper from responsible sources
FSC® C001701
www.fsc.org

Words in **bold** are explained in the glossary on page 22.

Picture credits
(t=top, b=bottom, l=left, r=right, c=center, bc=back cover, fc=front cover)

Alamy 1b Mike Stone; 9br Gale S.Hanratty/Alamy Stock Photo; 12br Dorling Kindersley Ltd/Alamy Stock Photo

Corbis 15r Simko

Getty 6r Rosemary Calvert; 17tr Ed Reschke

Hawk Conservancy Trust 14b

Nature Picture Library 4-5 Naturfoto Online; 17br Solvin Zanki; 19tr Marie Read; 20bl Stephen Dalton

Photolibrary Group 11br & 24 James Osmond; 21 Nick Cable

Science Photo Library 14-15 Bruno Petriglia; 16-17 Dr Jeremy Burgess

Shutterstock 2 Le Do; 5tr aleks.k; 4bl Vizerskaya; 6l Matt Benoit; 7l Fotoferner; 8-9 Little Adventures; 10b & 10t kaczor58; 11tl Fotofermer; 12t Jiang Hongyan; 12c & 23 Brzostowska; 12bl jopelka; 13 Pling; 18bl Giedriius; 18-19 Dudarev Mikhail; 20-21 Allen Paul Photography; bc Charged One; bc r 3523studio; bc l rsooll; fc jurgal

CONTENTS

WHAT IS AN OAK?

An oak is a type of tree. Oak trees live in forests, woods, gardens, and parks. They grow all over the world.

Trees are plants that grow tall. They have branches, where many leaves grow.

Trees have long roots that grow deep in the ground.

Roots take water from the ground.

A tree's stem is called a **trunk**. It is strong and covered in **bark**.

THE STORY OF AN OAK TREE

There are more than 600 different types of oak tree. All oak trees begin life as a small **acorn**.

A baby oak tree grows from the acorn. It takes many years for the small plant to grow into a tall tree.

1

An acorn is a **nut** with a seed inside it.

2

The first leaves begin to grow.

A young tree is called a **sapling**.

Now the tree is ready to make more seeds, so it grows lots of acorns. The story of how a small acorn grows into an oak tree is called a **life cycle**.

RIPE AND READY

An acorn grows in a little cup that hangs from the oak tree. Each oak tree grows thousands of acorns.

At the end of the summer, most of the acorns are **ripe** and ready to grow. Soon they will begin to fall from the tree.

It is **fall** and the oak leaves are changing color.

Ripe acorns are hard, smooth, and brown. There is food inside the acorns. It will help the new plants to grow.

The acorns from an English oak hang from little stalks.

This acorn is from the black oak, which only grows in North America.

ROOTS AND SHOOTS

The ripe acorns fall to the ground.

An acorn's hard skin begins to crack open and a small white root grows down into the **soil**. This is called **germination**.

An acorn needs air, water, and warmth to grow. Some acorns stay in the ground for years before they are ready to germinate. Others germinate in the fall, or in the spring.

2

The acorn opens up more, and a green shoot appears.

1

Roots grow into the soil to get water.

3

The first leaves grow and open.

A small green shoot grows up toward the sunlight and leaves appear.

4

The oak plant is still small. It is called a **seedling**.

GROWING UP

The young oak tree uses sunlight, water, and air to make its own food. It grows bigger and stronger every year, but most oak trees grow slowly.

This is the leaf of an English oak tree. Its lobes are large and rounded.

A sessile oak has lobes that are small and rounded.

This red oak leaf has pointed lobes.

A Hungarian oak leaf is long and thin with lots of deep lobes.

All trees have a crown. It is the part of the tree that has branches and leaves.

The trunk grows tall and thick. An oak tree has many big branches and they have many leaves.

This oak tree is more than 300 years old.

GROWING FLOWERS

It is spring and it is getting warmer. This is the time when many plants begin to grow flowers.

Most oak trees first grow flowers when they are about 20 years old. They grow flowers every year for the next 70 years, or more. An oak tree has two types of flowers.

Female flowers are tiny and they grow near the top of the oak tree's crown.

Male flowers are called **catkins**. Each catkin has a long stem with many small flowers growing on it.

The male flowers make a yellow dust called **pollen**.

HOW ACORNS GROW

It is a windy day and the wind blows the pollen off the catkins.

The pollen is carried by the wind. Some pollen lands on female flowers.

There are **eggs** growing inside the flowers. The pollen grows down until it reaches an egg. The pollen joins with the egg. This is called **fertilization**.

When an egg is fertilized it can grow into a seed, which is safe inside an acorn. The acorn is small but it will grow in the summer, and ripen.

The female flowers are growing into acorns.

This acorn has started to turn brown.

ON THE MOVE

The summer has ended and the tree is getting ready to rest for the winter. Some oak trees lose their leaves in the fall, but some types of oak are **evergreen**.

The acorns are ripe and full of food. Many animals visit oak forests to eat the acorns that fall to the ground.

Deer can digest acorns easily and they are a good source of protein for them.

Squirrels and birds carry acorns away and hide them. They will eat them in the long winter months, but if they forget to eat them the acorns may grow into new trees!

Acorn woodpeckers collect acorns from oak trees and store them in holes in the trunk.

GROWING OLD

An old oak tree is a home to many animals and plants.

Rabbits dig burrows around its roots, birds nest in its branches, and bugs hide under its leaves.

Wasp nest

Insects live in oak trees. Wasps chew the wood and use it to make their nests.

An oak tree can live for hundreds of years. Even when it dies it is still a home for animals, plants, and **fungi**.

Old oak trees are cut down for their wood, or **timber**.

Oak wood is used to make furniture, boats, and park benches.

GLOSSARY

Acorn
An oak seed.

Bark
The hard layer on the outside of a tree trunk.

Catkins
Male flowers on a tree.

Egg
The female part of a plant.

Evergreen
A plant that does not lose its leaves in fall.

Fall
The season that comes after summer and before winter.

Fertilization
When a grain of pollen joins with an egg.

Fungi
Mushrooms and toadstools are types of fungi.

Germination
When a seed begins to grow.

Life cycle
The story of how a living thing changes from birth to death, and how it has young, or makes seeds that grow into new plants.

Nut
A hard fruit with a seed inside.

Pollen
Yellow dust that is made by male flowers, or catkins.

Ripe
Ready to eat.

Sapling
A young tree with leaves.

Seedling
A young plant that has grown from a seed.

Soil
Where plants grow in the ground.

Timber
The wood from a tree that is used to make things.

Trunk
The woody stem of a tree.

INDEX

NOTES FOR PARENTS AND TEACHERS

- Look through the book and talk about the pictures. Read the captions and ask questions about the things in the photographs that have not been mentioned in the text.

- Help your child to find out more about plants and their life cycles with hands-on science. It is easy to grow most beans and many flower seeds, and watch their life cycles unfold in just one or two seasons.

- It is possible to germinate acorns and grow oak trees from them. The best way to do this is to research what types of oak grow well in your area, and what conditions those particular acorns need to germinate. Attempt to grow several trees, as not all will germinate or survive to the sapling stage.

- Visit woodlands together and talk about the habitat. Draw pictures or take photographs of animals and plants that live in a woodland habitat. Look out for the stages of plant life cycles, such as seeds, fruits, seedlings, and flowers.

- Make a family tree together and use it to talk about time and relationships. Children find it hard to imagine that adults were once young. Show them photographs, and share your memories of childhood, to help them to understand time, and how people change.